THE HEALING
JOURNAL

JOY MARGETTS

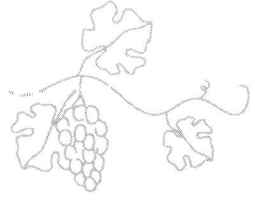

First published in Great Britain in 2022

Broad Place Publishing
83 Nettleham Road
Lincoln
LN2 1RU

The Healing Journal
ISBN 978-1-915-03480-9

For more information on Joy Margetts and her writing go to www.joymargetts.com

*You're my place of quiet retreat, and
your wraparound presence
becomes my shield as I wrap myself in
your Word!
Psalm 119:114 TPT*

READ * REST * PRAY * LISTEN * WRITE

A note from Joy:

I am so pleased that this journal has found its way into your hands. Pleased and excited, because journals have become such an important part of my own devotional life. A journal is simply a book that provides a space to write down your thoughts and prayers, to respond to what you have read or heard God speak to you. But I also I believe that this journal could become a space where you encounter God's healing for yourself.

God's Words are so powerful. I have proved that over and over in my own life. The truth of God's Word, and my choice to believe that truth, enabled God to do a healing work in me. That in turn lead me to write *The Healing*, which although fiction and set in another time and place, is really my story.

The words on these journal pages include quotes from *The Healing* that encapsulate some of the truths that God had to remind me of. And then there are words taken directly from scripture, words that have become a lifeline to me.

As you read and respond to these words, my prayer is that you will hear God speak clearly and lovingly to you. That He will cause hope to arise in you to believe in the God who speaks, and the God who heals.

'God's will is for you to live. Your life can have meaning and purpose. There is always hope while there is life. But you have to choose. To live, and to hope. Choose hope, and I have every belief that you will not regret the life God leads you into.'

The Healing p21

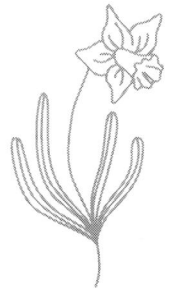

I have come that they may have life, and
that they may have it more abundantly
John 10:10 NKJV.

'I am urging you to choose hope. You can let the despair take you, or you can choose another way.'
'I know it seems an impossibility to you, that there could be something better for you than this life here and now. Or a life better than your life that has passed before. But surely choosing to believe there could be is better than believing that there definitely isn't...'

The Healing p29

*For I know the thoughts that I think
toward you, says the Lord,
thoughts of peace and not of evil, to give
you a future and a hope.*
Jeremiah 29:11 NKJV

'Being thankful is a good place to start in order to begin to see things more positively.
Be thankful for the everyday things, big and small. Focus your mind on those good things that you are grateful for.'

The Healing p29

*In everything give thanks; for this is the
will of God in Christ Jesus for you
I Thessalonians 5:18 NKJV.*

'The tree will bear fruit again. We have seen it so many times before to know that it is true. Spring always follows winter. While the tree lives, even through the winter, then there is hope that it will flourish again when spring comes.

So it is with us. We are sometimes defined, and altered, by the hard things that life throws at us, but we can learn to even appreciate the winter seasons.

It is often in those hard times that God is doing the deepest and most important things inside of us, to prepare us for the more fruitful seasons of our lives that will inevitably follow. Our responsibility is to make sure our roots are deep and grounded in truth. In God, and what He says.'

The Healing p34

*He will be standing firm like a flourishing
tree planted by God's design, deeply rooted
by the brooks of bliss, bearing fruit in every
season of life. He is never dry, never
fainting,
ever blessed, ever prosperous.*
Psalm 1:4 TPT

'...these seemingly dead peas have extraordinary life-giving potential. Within each of these peas is all that is needed to create a healthy fruit-bearing pea plant. They have to be buried, and watered and tended, but they will produce life from what seems to be dried up and dead.'

The Healing p42

*A single grain of wheat will never be
more than a single grain of wheat
unless it drops into the ground and
dies. Because then it sprouts and
produces a great harvest of wheat—all
because one grain died.*
John 12:24 TPT

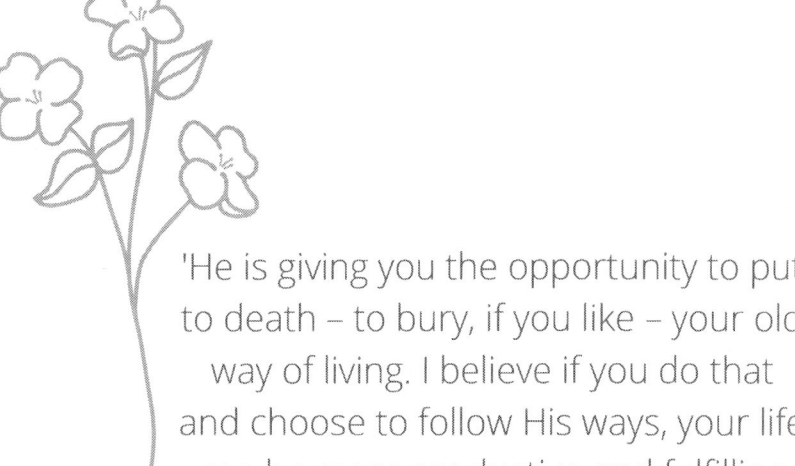

'He is giving you the opportunity to put to death – to bury, if you like – your old way of living. I believe if you do that and choose to follow His ways, your life can be more productive and fulfilling than you could ever imagine.'

The Healing p42

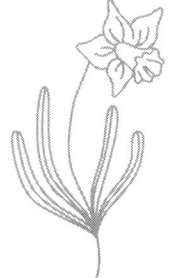

Then He said to them all, "If anyone desires to come after Me, let him deny himself, and take up his cross daily, and follow Me.
Luke 9:23 NKJV.

'Your mind and heart and spirit have
been wounded far more deeply than the
wounds of your flesh. That inner recovery
will take much longer, but I am confident
that God wants to see you fully healed.
He is the great redeemer and life
restorer, I can testify to that in my own
life.'

The Healing p47

He makes me to lie down in green
pastures;
He leads me beside the still waters.
He restores my soul;
Psalm 23:2-3 NKJV

'I can assure you,' Hywel continued, 'sitting here with you, that as sure as the sun there will set and rise again tomorrow, there is hope that you can walk free from all of it. From darkness, into life-giving light. That is the message of Easter is it not?'
I believe each of us can be free of the power of darkness, because of the resurrection. God offers forgiveness and light to us all.'

The Healing p57

But if we freely admit our sins when his light uncovers them, he will be faithful to forgive us every time. God is just to forgive us our sins because of Christ, and he will continue to cleanse us from all unrighteousness.

1 John 1:9 TPT

'We can all know God's love and blessing, but some of us choose to take what He has given us and squander it, while others live with ingratitude and a feeling of entitlement and self-righteousness. All He wants is for us to come back to Him with repentant hearts and He will embrace us and celebrate us, and restore us to right relationship with Him. Living as God's son in a close, love relationship with Him, is the absolute best. It is what we were designed for.'

The Healing p71

And he arose and came to his father. But when he was still a great way off, his father saw him and had compassion, and ran and fell on his neck and kissed him.
Luke 15:20 NKJV

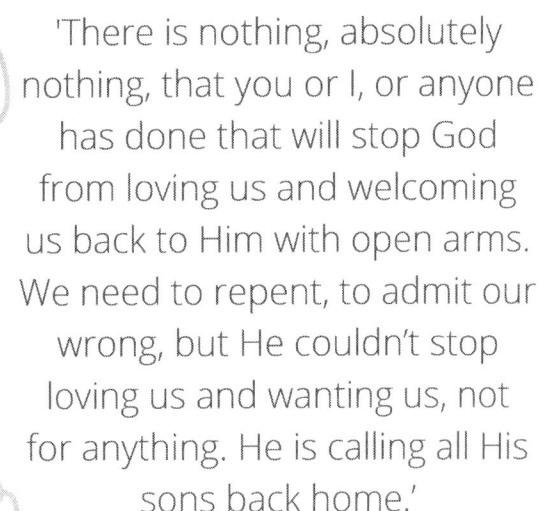

'There is nothing, absolutely nothing, that you or I, or anyone has done that will stop God from loving us and welcoming us back to Him with open arms. We need to repent, to admit our wrong, but He couldn't stop loving us and wanting us, not for anything. He is calling all His sons back home.'

The Healing p71

For I am persuaded that neither death nor life, nor angels nor principalities nor powers, nor things present nor things to come, nor height nor depth, nor any other created thing, shall be able to separate us from the love of God which is in Christ Jesus our Lord.

Romans 8:38-39 NKJV

Philip felt a growing excitement within him that hadn't been there before, and hope – yes, hope – that was not just of his own choosing. A knowing, a deep knowing that his life could now have meaning and purpose.

The Healing p78

Being confident of this very thing,
that He who has begun a good
work in you will complete it until
the day of Jesus Christ
Philippians 1:6 NKJV

'True worship is about our heart response to God. It should come out of a deep love for Him, and appreciation for all He has done for us. The form that worship takes is not restricted to singing or church services. It can be expressed in many different ways.'

The Healing p81

*God is Spirit, and those who
worship Him must worship in
spirit and truth.*
John 4:24 NKJV

'Every time we help someone else in Christ's name, especially when it inconveniences us, it is an act of worship. Every time we give our time, strength and minds to doing the things that God wants us to do, rather than doing what we would rather do, that is our sacrifice of praise to Him.'

The Healing p81

Beloved friends, what should be our proper response to God's marvelous mercies? To surrender yourselves to God to be his sacred, living sacrifices. And live in holiness, experiencing all that delights his heart. For this becomes your genuine expression of worship.

Romans 12:1 TPT

'It's amazing how the things around us can either make us feel at peace inside, or can steal our peace. Storms without can cause storms within.'

The Healing p94

I leave the gift of peace with you—my peace. Not the kind of fragile peace given by the world, but my perfect peace. Don't yield to fear or be troubled in your hearts—instead, be courageous!

John 12:27 TPT

'We choose to have faith in who God says He is, and what He is capable of. We can also take courage from who He says we are, His sons.
We can trust that He has plans for our lives, and He has the power to accomplish those things for us.'

The Healing p95

*For you did not receive the spirit of
bondage again to fear, but you received
the Spirit of adoption by whom we cry
out, "Abba, Father"*
Romans 8:15 NKJV

'We have no power... to fight on their behalf. But we did have the power to encourage and bless them, and we still have the power of prayer. We must trust that God will fight their battles and provide for them. We can also speak up if we hear false rumours and counter them with words of praise – we can trust their care to the Great Provider and Defender, but not forget the power of our prayers.'

The Healing p105

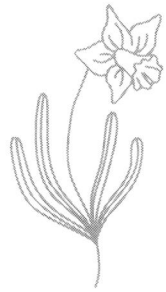

Don't be pulled in different directions or worried about a thing. Be saturated in prayer throughout each day, offering your faith-filled requests before God with overflowing gratitude. Tell him every detail of your life, then God's wonderful peace that transcends human understanding, will guard your heart and mind through Jesus Christ.
Philippians 4:6-7 TPT

'Indeed, you will meet monks, I am
afraid, who are religious in their
pious observance of the Rule, but
have no living relationship with God
to speak of.
False piety and religious observance
can be a pretence for a heart not
truly submitted to God.'

The Healing p108

The Lord does not see as man sees; for man looks at the outward appearance, but the Lord looks at the heart.
1 Samuel 16:7 NKJV

'God had different ideas. I've come a long way since my wild and headstrong days. I have learned a lot about myself, and I am now very content to be exactly where God wants me to be, and exactly all God says I am to be.'

The Healing p116

Find your delight and true pleasure in
Yahweh,
and he will give you what you desire the most.
Give God the right to direct your life,
and as you trust him along the way,
you'll find he pulled it off perfectly!
Psalm 37:4-5 TPT

'A far more wise and loving teacher... The Holy Spirit, God Himself, and I believe He has come to dwell inside of you.
It is He that has brought the change about, He who has created a new man inside of you, He who will continue to guide, and teach, and direct you as you follow this new path.
You do not have to fear what lies ahead for you, Philip, because He has promised to go before you, and prepare the way for you. It is a lot for you to understand at the moment, but I think you will more and more see His work in your life, grow to trust His ways, and hear Him speaking to you in the quiet of your heart.'

The Healing p132

And I will ask the Father and he will give you another Savior, the Holy Spirit of Truth, who will be to you a friend just like me—and he will never leave you. The world won't receive him because they can't see him or know him. But you know him intimately because he remains with you and will live inside you.

John 14 :16-17 TPT

'They could have let tragedy and heartbreak define them. They could have believed that they deserved to cling to the son they had fought to bring into the world. They could have fought back at God, and taken offence at Him for wanting their son. Instead they have shown only unconditional love, humility and grace. They epitomise God to me. Much more than many so-called men of God I have known.'

The Healing p137

Love suffers long and is kind; love does not envy; love does not parade itself, is not puffed up; does not behave rudely, does not seek its own, is not provoked, thinks no evil; does not rejoice in iniquity, but rejoices in the truth; bears all things, believes all things, hopes all things, endures all things.
1 Corinthians 13:4-7 NKJV

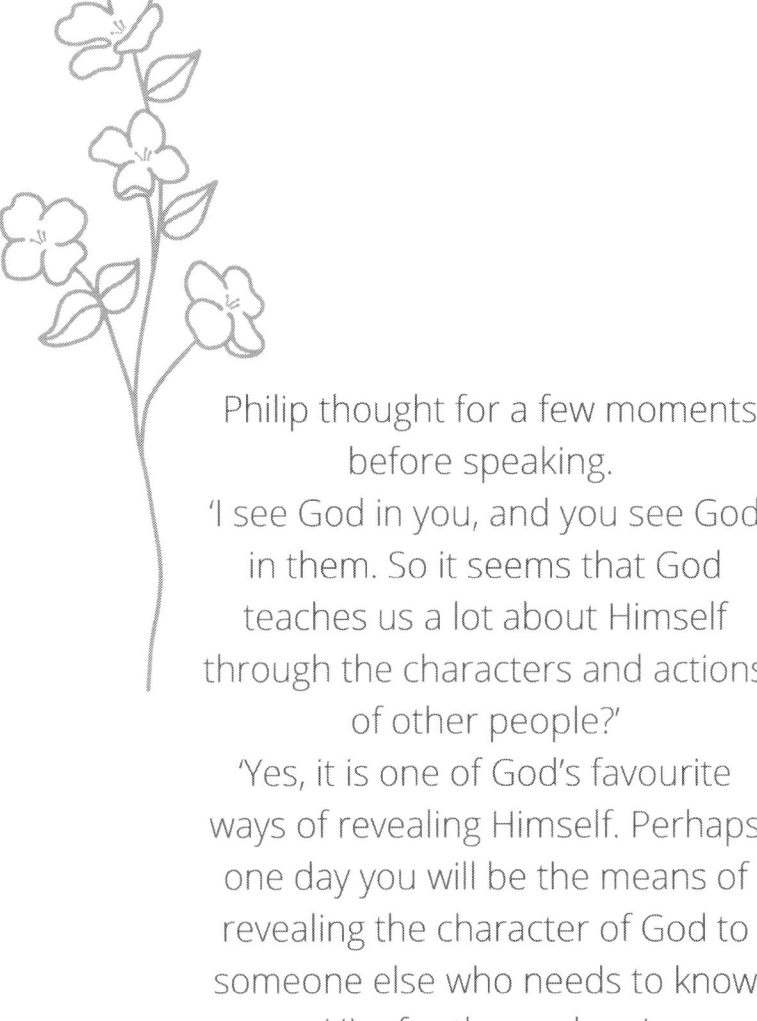

Philip thought for a few moments before speaking.
'I see God in you, and you see God in them. So it seems that God teaches us a lot about Himself through the characters and actions of other people?'
'Yes, it is one of God's favourite ways of revealing Himself. Perhaps one day you will be the means of revealing the character of God to someone else who needs to know Him for themselves.'

The Healing p137

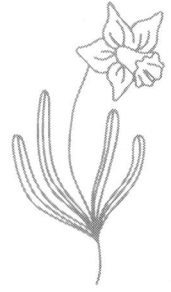

*Let every activity of your lives and
every word that comes from your lips
be drenched with the beauty of our
Lord Jesus, the Anointed One.*
Colossians 3:17 TPT

'A life devoted to God must be more than just private prayer and contemplation. It must look like something to others.
Our faith must work itself out in how we live towards one another. Living in community like this enables us to do that. To learn to serve one another, but also to learn how much we need each other.'

The Healing p148

Love empowers us to fulfill the law of the Anointed One as we carry each other's troubles. 3If you think you are somebody too important to stoop down to help another (when really you are not), you are living in deception.
Galatians 6:2-3 TPT

'Many of us grow up believing we are self-sufficient and don't need other people. We learn to rely on ourselves and not to trust others, often through painful experiences. We may even begin to resent others interfering in our lives...

...We serve one another and we also make room in our lives and work for others to serve us. It's learning that we cannot operate in isolation, and that people have been placed in our lives by God to enrich our lives, and to show us more about ourselves, and ultimately about Him.'

The Healing p149

*Always give thanks to Father God for
every person he brings into your life in the
name of our Lord Jesus Christ.
And out of your reverence for Christ be
supportive of each other in love.*
Ephesians 5:20-21 TPT

'Every time I finish an illustration, I feel such a sense of completeness. Like I have found some purpose to my day. Like I have been able to offer something of some worth back to God, and to His people.'
'Creativity allows us to do that. It draws on His beauty and it produces things that glorify Him. A form of worship in itself, even, if done with the right motives.'

The Healing p150

"You are worthy, O Lord,
To receive glory and honor and power;
For You created all things,
And by Your will they exist and were
created."
Revelation 4:11 NKJV

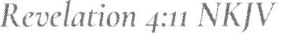

Now as he read the Psalms, it was the cries of praise, the promises of hope, and the testimonies to God's faithfulness that spoke most into his situation. He could meditate on these, and hear God's voice speaking into his spirit and soul.
He loved the Gospels also, and these he found himself reading as he was illuminating them, his pen being put to one side as the story of his Saviour gripped his heart. The man Jesus came to life in the words, and made him yearn to live a life modelled on His.'

The Healing p151

How sweet are Your words to my taste,
Sweeter than honey to my mouth!
Psalm 119:103 NKJV

Aware of only the sound of his own breathing and the feel of the warm sunshine as it kissed his shoulder, Philip stayed bowed and let God's peace flow over him. It was as if his soul breathed deeply, and found its way back to rest. Philip smiled to himself. It was so much easier these days, in this place, in this atmosphere, to recentre himself and let peace and joy quieten the tumult within. He thanked God for teaching him the simplicity of a devoted life, through the example and compassion of the true lovers of God that had become his teachers in this place.

The Healing p159

God, hear my prayer. Listen to my heart's cry.
For no matter where I am,
even when I'm far from home,
I will cry out to you for a father's help.
When I'm feeble and overwhelmed by life,
guide me into your glory, where I am safe and
sheltered.
Psalm 61:1-2 TPT

She was standing in front of the high altar, her face lifted up to the light streaming through the great windows, tears glistening on her cheeks. Her hands were clasped together in prayer but her back stood erect, as if she approached God as an honoured daughter and not some snivelling sinner. She spoke to God as if she knew Him intimately, pouring out her heart to Him like the psalmist of old.

The Healing p160

So now we draw near freely and boldly to where grace is enthroned, to receive mercy's kiss and discover the grace we urgently need to strengthen us in our time of weakness.

Hebrews 4:16 TPT

'My heart has learned not to carry the griefs and cares of this world, rather to leave them at the altar, and accept God's peace in place of them. I don't need to come to a physical altar to do that, but needed to escape the noise and company just for a moment. And I was drawn into this beautiful sanctuary.'

The Healing p160

So here's what I've learned through it all: Leave all your cares and anxieties at the feet of the Lord, and measureless grace will strengthen you.
Psalm 55:22 TPT

'He still loved me deeply, and he saw that my guilt would destroy my life if I didn't deal with it. "I forgive you,"' he said. "Now you must learn to forgive yourself." It didn't take me long to realise that in what Cenred had done for me was a living example of how God forgives, Philip.

He loves us so much that He is willing to forgive us over and over again. He gave us His Son so that we can live guilt-free. We confess our sins and He forgives us, absolves us freely. I learned too that forgiveness, forgiving others, is one of the most powerful keys we have to unlock chains of guilt, offence and anger in our own lives.'

The Healing p184

Then Peter came to Him and said, "Lord, how often shall my brother sin against me, and I forgive him? Up to seven times?"
Jesus said to him, "I do not say to you, up to seven times, but up to seventy times seven."
Matthew 18:21-22 NKJV

'If I was to throw a hook and line into this river and catch a fish,' said Hywel, 'when I landed it, I would take the hook out of its mouth.
When we forgive someone who has hurt us, it is not letting them off the hook, or in any way minimising the wrong they have caused us, because they will have to face both the consequences of sin, and the judgement of God for their wrong actions if they do not repent.

Forgiving someone is actually taking the hook out of our own mouths – or out of our own hearts, perhaps.
If left in place, that hook can fester, leading to offence, bitterness, hatred, anger and revenge, leading us into making more wrong decisions, causing more hurt.'

The Healing p184

In every relationship be swift to choose peace over competition, and run swiftly toward holiness, for those who are not holy will not see the Lord. Watch over each other to make sure that no one misses the revelation of God's grace. And make sure no one lives with a root of bitterness sprouting within them which will only cause trouble and poison the hearts of many.

Hebrews 12:14-16 TPT

'I think you have to consider, Philip, whether it is only fear stopping you from taking what God is offering you, and grasping it with both hands? If it is fear, then you need to just step through it. I believe that you will find, if you do, that what you feared most was merely an illusion.'

The Healing p205

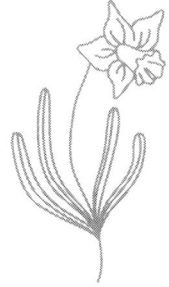

For God has not given us a spirit of fear, but of power and of love and of a sound mind.
2Timothy 1:7 NKJV

'You can still live a life of devotion to Him, brother, out there in the world. You can still serve Him in serving others.

In telling your story, you can instil hope in the hopeless. In loving others as you have been loved, they too can experience the love of God. Caring for the poor and needy, sharing your life and sharing your faith – you don't need an abbey church, or a cloister, or a monk's habit to do those things. Nor do you need prayer offices, and rules and vows. I think, Philip, you are called to live a different life to us here. But a life as much devoted to God as ours is.'

The Healing p206

For you, brethren, have been called to liberty; only do not use liberty as an opportunity for the flesh, but through love serve one another.
Galatians 5:13 NKJV

'I believe God will give you the right words to say in this situation. He promises us Holy Spirit wisdom when we ask for it. In fact, He is wisdom itself, and you, my brother, are wiser than you give yourself credit for. Between you and God, I trust that you will know what to do, when the time is right to do it. God will go before you and will be with you, and He will be in you.'

The Healing p207

If any of you lacks wisdom, let him ask of God, who gives to all liberally and without reproach, and it will be given to him.

James 1:5 NKJV

'I thought I owed God my whole life, and that meant inside these abbey walls. I have come to see that devotion to God, a lifetime of devotion to Him, can take many forms, not all requiring separation from the world.'

God does not want empty, meaningless offerings made out of compulsion; rather, He wants hearts of thanksgiving and praise, and lives lived righteously. If we live this way, we are truly fulfilling our vows to Him.'

The Healing p214

The thief does not come except to steal, and to kill, and to destroy. I have come that they may have life, and that they may have it more abundantly.
John 10:10 NKJV

If using this journal has blessed you I would love to hear from you.
You can contact me via my website at www.joymargetts.com.

On my website you can also sign up to receive regular updates about me and my writing, and read more about my books and the stories behind them.

I would love to make contact with you there.

With special thanks to Joy Velykorodnyy and Broad Place Publishing

Also by Joy Margetts

www.joymargetts.com

Printed in Poland
by Amazon Fulfillment
Poland Sp. z o.o., Wrocław
15 October 2022

c6981f2a-e713-4f61-aaf5-1af6e902bf14R01